# Muslim Baby Book

## Keep a Record of Your Baby's Special Moments

Goodword

# بِسْمِ اللّٰهِ

**Bismillahirrahmanirrahim**

In the name of Allah, the Most Gracious, the Most Merciful

وَٱللَّهُ أَخۡرَجَكُم مِّنۢ بُطُونِ أُمَّهَٰتِكُمۡ
لَا تَعۡلَمُونَ شَيۡـٔٗا وَجَعَلَ لَكُمُ ٱلسَّمۡعَ
وَٱلۡأَبۡصَٰرَ وَٱلۡأَفۡـِٔدَةَ لَعَلَّكُمۡ تَشۡكُرُونَ ٧٨

"Allah brought you forth from the wombs of your mothers while you knew nothing, and gave you hearing and sight and hearts, so that you might be grateful."

*(Al-Nahl, 16:78)*

Baby book from:

________________

________________

Date of birth:

________________

________________

وَوَصَّيْنَا ٱلْإِنسَٰنَ بِوَٰلِدَيْهِ إِحْسَٰنًا ۖ حَمَلَتْهُ أُمُّهُۥ كُرْهًا وَوَضَعَتْهُ كُرْهًا ۖ وَحَمْلُهُۥ
وَفِصَٰلُهُۥ ثَلَٰثُونَ شَهْرًا ۚ حَتَّىٰٓ إِذَا بَلَغَ أَشُدَّهُۥ وَبَلَغَ أَرْبَعِينَ سَنَةً قَالَ رَبِّ
أَوْزِعْنِىٓ أَنْ أَشْكُرَ نِعْمَتَكَ ٱلَّتِىٓ أَنْعَمْتَ عَلَىَّ وَعَلَىٰ وَٰلِدَىَّ وَأَنْ أَعْمَلَ صَٰلِحًا
تَرْضَىٰهُ وَأَصْلِحْ لِى فِى ذُرِّيَّتِىٓ ۖ إِنِّى تُبْتُ إِلَيْكَ وَإِنِّى مِنَ ٱلْمُسْلِمِينَ ﴿١٥﴾

“We have enjoined on man kindness to his parents: his mother bore him, in pain and in pain she gave birth to him, and his bearing and weaning takes thirty months. At length, when he reaches the age of full maturity and attains forty years, he says, ‘O my Lord! Help me to be grateful for Your favours which You have bestowed upon me, and upon both my parents, and to do good deeds that will please You. Grant me righteousness in my offspring. Truly, I have turned to You and, truly, I submit to You.’”

*(Al-Ahqaf 46:15)*

# First message from birth

Date:

Time:

Day:

Place:

My feelings:

Reaction of the family:

The first one to hear it:

# Preparation for my arrival

وَٱخۡفِضۡ لَهُمَا جَنَاحَ ٱلذُّلِّ مِنَ
ٱلرَّحۡمَةِ وَقُل رَّبِّ ٱرۡحَمۡهُمَا
كَمَا رَبَّيَانِي صَغِيرٗا ٢٤

"...and treat them with humility and tenderness and say, 'Lord, be merciful to them both, as they raised me up when I was little.'"

*Al-Isra 17:24*

Furnishing of my room:

_______________

_______________

The first items that were bought:

_______________________________________

_______________________________________

_______________________________________

# My family

وَٱلَّذِينَ يَقُولُونَ رَبَّنَا هَبْ لَنَا
مِنْ أَزْوَٰجِنَا وَذُرِّيَّٰتِنَا قُرَّةَ
أَعْيُنٍ وَٱجْعَلْنَا لِلْمُتَّقِينَ إِمَامًا ﴿٧٤﴾

"...who say, 'Lord, grant us joy in our wives and children and make us a model for the righteous.'."

*(Al-Furqan, 25:74)*

My mother's name is:

---------------

---------------

My father's name is:

---------------

---------------

My brother's name is:

---------------

---------------

My sister's name is:

---------------

---------------

*Children are the flowers of Allah.

# My birth

Time: ____________

Day: ____________

Date: ____________

Place: ____________

## Why am I in the world?

وَمَا خَلَقْتُ ٱلْجِنَّ وَٱلْإِنسَ إِلَّا لِيَعْبُدُونِ ٥٦

"I created the jinn and mankind only so that they might worship Me."

(Al-Dhariyat 51:56)

# My first picture

Date: ______________________

Time: ______________________

Day: ______________________

Place: ______________________

# My first presents

My first presents were:

Photo of first gift

# What name has been chosen for me?

"A child has the right to be given a good meaningful name by his parents and to be taught good manners."

*Baihaqi*

Mom and Dad shortlisted the following names:

Boy's names:

Girl's names:

Eventually they have called me:

My name means:

# My appearance

"The best gift from a father to his child is education and upbringing."

*Tirmidhi*

I am a (gender):

The colour of my eye is:

The colour of my hair is:

The colour of my skin is:

My weight is:

My height is:

My parents' nationality is:

# The adhan and the iqamah

The one who read the *adhan* and the *iqamah* in my ears is:

-----------------------------------------------

-----------------------------------------------

The *adhan* and *iqamah* are not the Prophet's sunnah. It is in worldwide use among Muslims. Scholars believe this is not a bad habit because the *adhans* contain the *iqamah*, the most beautiful words, and tell us what the purpose of human life is..

وَقَالَ رَبِّ أَوْزِعْنِيٓ أَنْ أَشْكُرَ نِعْمَتَكَ
ٱلَّتِيٓ أَنْعَمْتَ عَلَيَّ وَعَلَىٰ وَٰلِدَيَّ وَأَنْ أَعْمَلَ
صَٰلِحًا تَرْضَىٰهُ وَأَدْخِلْنِي بِرَحْمَتِكَ
فِي عِبَادِكَ ٱلصَّٰلِحِينَ ﴿١٩﴾

"'Lord, inspire me to be thankful for the blessings You have granted me and my parents, and to do good deeds that please You; and include me, by Your grace, among Your righteous servants!'"

*(Al-Naml 27:19)*

# The Prophet's Sunnah at birth

"Among the believers who show the most perfect faith are those who have the best disposition and are kindest to their families."

*Tirmidhi*

The one who did *Tahnik* with a date and honey:

The weight of my shaved hair (on the occasion of *Aqiqa*) is:

The *Aqiqa* party was held on:

My name was given on the:

# My motorcycle

The first time that I could ride it was:

______________________________

The first time I could sit up was:

______________________________

I could crawl when I was:

______________________ months

I could stand when I was:

______________________ months

I could walk when I was:

______________________ months

I got my first tooth at:

______________________ months

# Food

The first thing I could eat was:

My most favourite food was:

What I did not want to eat was:

I could say *bismillah* for the first time when I was:

# My first words

اللّٰه

The first word I could say was:

________________

I could say "Allah" when I was:

________________

I could say *Bismillah* when I was:

________________

I could say Mom or Dad when I was:

________________

I could say *Alhamdulillah* when I was:

________________

I could say *Assalamu Alaykum* when I was:

________________

بِسْمِ اللّٰه

I could say the *Shahadah* when I was:

________________

I could read the first surah of the Quran when I was:

________________

# When I was 1 year old

"Paradise lies under the feet of the mother."

*Nasaï*

My height was: ____________________

My weight was: ____________________

Photo............first gift

Cute memories of Mom:

_______________________________________

_______________________________________

_______________________________________

_______________________________________

Cute memories of Dad:

_______________________________________

_______________________________________

_______________________________________

_______________________________________

# Some firsts for me

I first visited the mosque when I was:

I first saw snow when I was:

I offered my first prayer when I was:

I received my first prayer clothes when I was:

# My favourite toys

The nicest toy
I played with was:

______________

______________

The toys that I learnt
the most from were:

______________

______________

The one toy I really
wanted

______________

# Eid al-Adha

During Eid al-Adha
I was:

On this day we
went to:

We were visited by:

I received the
following gifts:

# Ramadan and Eid al-Fitr

يَٰٓأَيُّهَا ٱلَّذِينَ ءَامَنُواْ كُتِبَ عَلَيۡكُمُ ٱلصِّيَامُ كَمَا
كُتِبَ عَلَى ٱلَّذِينَ مِن قَبۡلِكُمۡ لَعَلَّكُمۡ تَتَّقُونَ ١٨٣

"Believers, fasting has been prescribed for you, just as it was prescribed for those before you, so that you may guard yourselves against evil."

*(Al-Baqarah, 2:183)*

During Eid al-Fitr I was:

______________________________

On this day we went to:

________________________________________

________________________________________

We were visited by:

________________________________________

________________________________________

I received the following gifts:

________________________________________

________________________________________

# My first drawing

# My first handprint

# Nice memories

Photo ...........months

Photo ...........months

Photo ...........months

Photo ...........months

Photo ...........months

Photo ...........months

# Advice from the Prophet Muhammad ﷺ

## About the Prayer (*Salah*)

The Prophet Muhammad ﷺ said: "Invite your children to say their prayers once they are seven years old. Dress them in trousers at the age of ten. And divide their beds."

(Abu Dawud)

## Being just to your children

Fear Allah and be just to your children...

(Bukhari)

## Treat your children equally

A man was sitting with the Prophet Muhammad ﷺ when his son came to him. The man kissed and hugged his son and seated him on his lap. Then his daughter came to him but he ignored her and did not seat her on his lap. The Prophet noticed this and said to him, "You should treat your children equally!"

(Al-Haythami, Majma 'Az-Zawaid 8/156)

## Teach your child the Quran

The Messenger of Allah said, "The best of you are those who learn the Quran and teach it."

(Muslim)

# Some advice from the Quran

"Luqman said to his son, counselling him, 'My son, do not associate anything with Allah. Associating others with Him is a terrible wrong.'

"We have enjoined man to show kindness to his parents—for his mother bears him, in hardship upon hardship, and his weaning takes two years. [We said] Give thanks to Me and to your parents; all will return to Me. But if they press you to associate something with Me about which you have no knowledge, do not obey them. Yet be kind to them in this world and follow the path of those who turn to Me. You will all return to Me in the end, and I will tell you everything that you have done.

[Luqman further said,] 'O my son! Though it be but the weight of a grain of mustard seed and though it be hidden in a rock, or in the heavens or on the earth, Allah will bring it forth. Truly, Allah is the knower of all subtleties and He is aware. O my dear son! Say your prayers regularly, and enjoin good, and forbid evil, and endure patiently whatever may befall you. Surely, this is something which requires firm resolve. Do not avert your face from people out of haughtiness and do not walk with pride on the earth: for, behold, Allah does not love arrogant and boastful people. Walk modestly and lower your voice, for the ugliest of all voices is the braying of the ass.'”

*(Luqman, 31:13-19)*

First Published in 2018


Art editor: Mateen Ahmad
Graphic design: K.K. Sahadevan
Illustrator: Gurmeet

Goodword Books
A-21, Sector 4, Noida-201301, India
Tel. +9111-46010170, +9111-49534795
Mob. +91-8588822672
email: info@goodwordbooks.com
www.goodwordbooks.com

Printed in India